UNCOVERING AMERICAN HISTORY™

A PRIMARY SOURCE INVESTIGATION OF ELLIS ISLAND

CAITLIN MERRICK AND
GILLIAN HOUGHTON

rosen publishing's
rosen central

Published in 2016 by The Rosen Publishing Group, Inc.
29 East 21st Street, New York, NY 10010

First Edition

Library of Congress Cataloging-in-Publication Data

Merrick, Caitlin.
A primary source investigation of Ellis Island/Caitlin Merrick and Gillian Houghton.—First edition.
pages cm.—(Uncovering American history)
Includes bibliographical references and index.
ISBN 978-1-4994-3505-4 (library bound)
1. Ellis Island Immigration Station (N.Y. and N.J.)—History–Sources—Juvenile literature. 2. United States—Emigration and immigration—History—Sources—Juvenile literature. 3. United States—Emigration and immigration—Government policy—History–Sources—Juvenile literature. I. Houghton, Gillian. II. Title.
JV6484.M47 2015
325.73–dc23

2014041870

Manufactured in the United States of America

CONTENTS

INTRODUCTION

Between 1892 and 1954, more than twelve million immigrants came to the United States through Ellis Island. This small island in New York Harbor started out as a mere 3.5 acres (1.4 hectares) but later enlarged to 27.5 acres (11 ha) to become one of the most-used immigration stations in the United States. Nearly half of the European immigrants came through Ellis Island, with the Statue of Liberty standing above them. "The New Colossus," a poem by Emma Lazarus is carved on the pedestal of the Statue of Liberty and greets every visitor to New York Harbor with the words:

> Give me your tired, your poor,
> Your huddled masses yearning to breathe free,
> The wretched refuse of your teeming shore.
> Send these, the homeless, tempest-tost to me,
> I lift my lamp beside the golden door!

The promise of liberty led hopeful and often desperate travelers to leave their homes and

An aerial view of Ellis Island

immigrate to the United States. Most prospective Americans traveled to America through New York's Battery Park in the south of Manhattan, making New York Harbor the single largest port of entry for these prospective Americans. Ellis Island became the immigration station for New York after 1892, though technically the island is in New Jersey.

In this sixty-two-year period when Ellis Island operated as an immigration station, about 12 million of the 25.5 million American immigrants passed through Ellis Island.

Immigration continues to be a vibrant force in American culture today, even though, as in the earliest days of Ellis Island, the government's immigration policies are fiercely debated. Consider Miami's Little Haiti; the Islamic community of Dearborn, Michigan; San Francisco's Chinatown; or the West Indian community of Brooklyn, New York. These communities tell a varied history of immigration and share a collective part in the American story. The history of Ellis Island, which today serves as an immigration museum, uncovers American diversity and shows powerful images and telling accounts of the people who belong inside of America's family album.

★ CHAPTER ONE

AN ISLAND OF NO INTEREST

The future site of Ellis Island was just a muddy, 3-acre (1 ha) sandbank in the early 1660s that barely rose above the waters of the harbor during high tide. When the first Dutch colonists arrived in New Amsterdam (later, New York), this sandy patch of land in the middle of the Hudson River was notable only for its rich oyster beds and for the schools of shad (a fish related to the herring) that swam past its shores. The water was too shallow for ships to dock near it. There was little vegetation on the ground that managed to

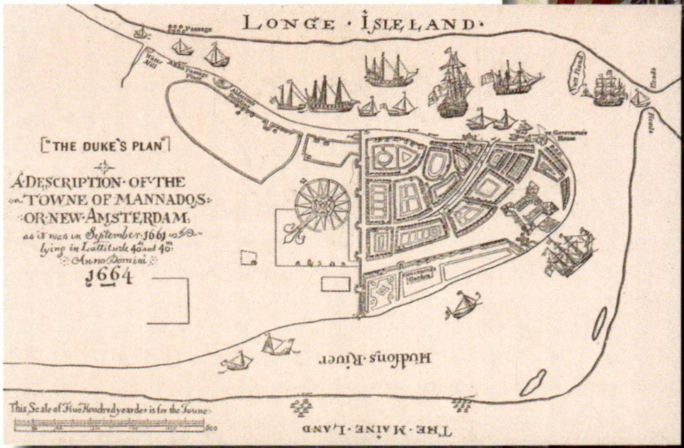

This map of New York City in 1664 is known as *The Duke's Plan: A description of the Towne of Mannados or New Amsterdam*. It was presented to James, Duke of York, shortly after the English captured the city from the Dutch and renamed it after the duke.

stay above the tides. It was an island of little interest to anybody.

CHANGING HANDS

In the course of its unimpressive early history, the island had many different names and owners. It was known variously as Dyre's Island, Bucking Island, Gibbet Island, and Oyster Island. It earned its modern name after Samuel Ellis, the island's only known eighteenth-century owner, who bought the property sometime before 1785. When Ellis died in 1794, the island was willed to a grandson, who soon died as well. Ownership of the property passed among the members of the Ellis family for the following decade. Though privately owned, Ellis Island had become home to an army battery (a fort housing artillery pieces, such as cannons, that were used to defend the surrounding land and waterways).

In 1794, with the threat of war with France looming, the United States government sought to construct a series of defensive fortifications in New York Harbor. The army's chief of engineers chose Ellis Island, along with neighboring Bedloe's Island and Governor's Island, as the main sites of military operations. Construction of defensive works proceeded on the island over the next decade. In 1807, the state of New York began proceedings to purchase Ellis Island in its entirety for military purposes. New York deeded the property to the federal government the following year.

While military construction proceeded on Bedloe's Island and Governor's Island, sandy terrain prevented the building of anything substantial on Ellis Island. The army's original plans were scrapped. Instead, it built a small battery with room for only twenty guns, which was completed just before the outbreak of the War of 1812. During this conflict

A hand-colored woodcut of Ellis Island in the 1870s before the immigration center was built

between the United States and Great Britain, Ellis Island supported a small garrison (a military post housing troops) but saw no active combat.

The following decades were uneventful on Ellis Island. It was occasionally used as the site of executions and as an army recruitment depot until 1835, when the U.S. Navy occupied the island and installed a powder magazine—a storage facility for thousands of barrels of gunpowder. This arsenal was handed over to the U.S. Army when that branch of the military was given control of the island in 1841. A small navy guard, however, continued to protect and maintain the magazine over the next three decades. Additional defensive works were constructed during the Civil War, and the stockpile of weapons and gunpowder grew. At the end of the war and again several years later, public outcry rose up against the possible dangers of such a large quantity of explosive material gathered in a place so close to New York City and Jersey City, New Jersey. Nothing was done about it, however, until 1890, when

ISLAND OF GULLS AND OYSTERS

Around 1630, the colonial governors of what was then called Nieuw Amsterdam, bought a tiny mud bank near the New Jersey shore. At 3.5 acres (1.4 ha), it was of little use. The island barely rose above the surface of the water at high tide. The Native Americans called it Kioshk, or Gull Island, as gulls were its only inhabitants. The island was also surrounded by oyster beds, so the Dutch settlers gave it another name: Oyster Island.

ever-growing waves of immigration aroused a new interest in the possible usefulness of the muddy strip of unfertile land that was Ellis Island.

EARLY U.S. IMMIGRATION POLICY

Since 1855, New York City had welcomed its new immigrants at Castle Garden on the Battery in lower Manhattan, where a staff of state employees recorded their arrivals. Beginning in 1875, however, the federal government began taking a more active role in regulating and overseeing immigration. That year several nationwide immigration laws were enacted, aimed primarily at excluding criminals and prostitutes. Additional legislation in 1882 expanded the list of undesirable immigrants to include "any convict, lunatic, idiot, or any person unable to take care of himself or herself without becoming a public charge" (as quoted in Thomas Monroe Pitkin's *Keepers of the Gate*). Another law passed the same year—the Chinese Exclusion Act—excluded Chinese laborers who were thought to be stealing jobs from American workers. In 1885, the Alien Contract Labor Law was passed in order to protect the jobs and wages of American workers. It forbade American employers from recruiting foreign workers (who were willing to work for low wages) and paying for their passage.

An 1848 illustration of the Battery and Castle Gardens

Along with the U.S. government's new involvement in immigration policy came the creation of a federally structured immigration system. The secretary of the U.S. Treasury, in cooperation with state officials, was now given the responsibility of enforcing immigration law and overseeing the state employees. When the state commissioners at Castle Garden failed to enforce the law, federal labor inspectors had to be stationed there to insure compliance, further cementing the joint federal-state system of immigration regulation that was developing in New York.

Nearly as soon as this joint federal-state system was up and running, it became the target of angry newspaper editorials and a major source of embarrassment for the Treasury Department. In 1888, Congress created a committee to look into the management of the nation's immigration stations, specifically New York's Castle Garden, through which the majority of the country's immigrants passed. That year, 546,889 immigrants landed in the United States; of that number, 418,423 landed at the port of New York. Following the congressional investigation, the inspectors at Castle Garden were accused of emotionally and physically abusing the immigrants and extorting money from them. In addition, inspectors were failing to properly enforce federal immigration laws by allowing unfit immigrants into the United States.

Only a few months later, after another investigation into the Castle Garden immigration office revealed serious examples of mismanagement and corruption, the secretary of the treasury ended the arrangement between the federal and state immigration commissioners. The federal government, represented by the treasury secretary, would now have sole responsibility for processing immigrants at Castle Garden.

One of the treasury secretary's first decisions was to build an immigration station in New York City large enough to handle the ever-increasing number of immigrants flocking to America through New York Harbor. The treasury secretary proposed Bedloe's Island—home of the Statue of Liberty—as the new site. The *New York World* responded to the secretary's proposal with an angry editorial. The newspaper argued that the island, which "was to have been made into a beautiful park as a fit setting for the great Statue," would "be converted instead into a Babel," the chaotic biblical city in which the people suddenly began to speak many different languages and were no longer able to understand each other (according to Pitkin's *Keepers of the Gate*).

A later editorial in the same newspaper argued that the idea of an immigration station on "Liberty Island" was "universally deprecated [strongly disapproved of] by those who look with pride upon Liberty's imposing beacon," as quoted by Pitkin. Americans, though fiercely proud of their shared history of liberty and equality, were wary of the growing tide of eastern and southern European immigrants, people believed to be of lesser quality than the earlier waves of northern and western European immigrants. The *World*'s editorials accurately reflected this odd mix of patriotism and nativism (a favoring of earlier settlers over recent immigrants) in the late 1880s.

This controversial problem needed to be addressed, and Congress looked for a new location for the federal immigration station as a means to solve it. The need to protect the arsenal at Governor's Island and the need to remove the powder magazine from Ellis Island made the decision easier. The tiny patch of land between New York and New Jersey would become the main gateway to America.

★ CHAPTER TWO

THE "GOLDEN DOOR" OPENS

In 1890, the New York immigration station at Castle Garden closed. The federal government, now in control of immigration, appropriated $75,000 for construction at Ellis Island beginning in the spring of 1890. It was completed in January 1892. Wells were dug, and the island's size doubled to over 6 acres (2.4 ha) thanks to landfill created from ships' ballast and the excavation of subway tunnels in New York City. The final construction included more than 850 feet (259 meters) of docks, a large two-story main building, separate hospital buildings, a boiler house, a laundry facility, bathhouses, and an electric plant, all made of wood.

Construction workers on Ellis Island working on a building. The wooden structures would prove disastrous later on.

NEW IMMIGRATION CENTER, NEW POLICIES

As Ellis Island was under construction so, too, was a new legislative framework for processing immigrants and keeping out the "undesirable element," which was increasingly described in ethnic terms. Hungarians, Lithuanians, Russians (especially Russian Jews fleeing the oppression of the dictatorial czar), and Italians were believed to be ignorant, socially backward, and strange looking when compared to the Irish, British, German, and Scandinavian immigrants who came to America just a generation before.

Ethnic prejudice was not the only reason for the new immigrants' hostile reception in the United States. The more established northern European immigrants feared the arrival of a labor force willing to work for less than they were. This would decrease the number of jobs available and drive down wages. In 1891, Congress passed new immigration legislation in response to the complaints of the Knights of Labor, among other nativist labor organizations. Its restrictive provisions were designed to stem the tide of immigration, thereby protecting Americans' jobs. The law placed immigration at all ports of entry entirely under federal control. It required steamship companies to transport, at the companies' expense, any immigrants rejected by U.S. immigration authorities back to their country of origin. It added to the list of excluded aliens "persons suffering from a loathsome or dangerous contagious disease."

With these new regulations at his disposal, the commissioner of Ellis Island, Colonel John B. Weber, welcomed the station's first immigrant, Annie Moore, on

January 1, 1892. Immigration declined steadily in the course of the next five years, however, partly because of a cholera epidemic (a severe intestinal disease) in Europe, and the new immigration station was rarely crowded. Then, on June 14, 1897, a fire erupted in one of the station buildings, and only an hour later, according to some accounts, the entire compound was in ashes. No one was hurt, but nearly all of the records detailing the arrivals of hundreds of thousands of immigrants in New York between the years 1855 and 1897 were lost in the blaze.

Immigration officials set up temporary operations at the barge office in lower Manhattan, and, only a month later, builders began constructing a new, more fireproof station at Ellis Island. New York City sponsored a design contest to determine which architecture firm would win the new construction job. The winning design belonged to the firm of Boring and Tilton, known mainly for its work on public libraries nationwide. The main building, of red brick with limestone trim, was to be situated at the center of the island. It would have a commanding presence, with three high-arched windows above the entrances on the east and west sides and spired towers at each corner. To the north of the main building would be the restaurant, laundry facility, bathhouse, and power plant. On a newly created island across from the ferry slip, a hospital would be built. These designs quickly became a reality, and the new station was completed in 1900, for a total cost of $1.5 million.

ABUSE OF POWER

Though the new complex seemed to promise a fresh start for the United States' principal immigration center, from its

ANNIE MOORE

Annie Moore is immortalized in bronze both in New York Harbor and her native Ireland. She is believed to be the first person to arrive and be officially registered at Ellis Island. Moore arrived on January 1, 1892–her fifteenth birthday–with her two brothers. She was given a $10 gold piece by the superintendent of immigration, which she swore she would always keep as a memento. Moore married a bakery clerk and had eleven children. They lived on the Lower East Side of Manhattan.

This statue depicts Annie Moore and her brothers arriving at Ellis Island.

A 1903 photograph showing President Theodore Roosevelt (***second from right***) visiting Ellis Island. Roosevelt was determined to end corruption at Ellis Island, such as inspectors demanding bribes from immigrants, and appointed William Williams (***far right***) as the commissioner of Ellis Island.

first days, scandal plagued the new station at Ellis Island. Accusations quickly resurfaced that immigrants were being robbed, swindled, and abused by the station staff. In 1901, investigations revealed that steamship captains and immigration inspectors were selling U.S. citizenship papers to newly arrived immigrants, which would allow them to bypass inspection at Ellis Island. It was estimated that perhaps ten thousand foreigners had entered New York in this way.

Later that year, President Theodore Roosevelt set about reforming the immigration machine at Ellis Island, beginning by hiring a new commissioner of immigration. Roosevelt chose a Wall Street lawyer named William Williams who introduced sweeping reforms at Ellis Island and shepherded the station through one of the most populous immigration waves in American history. Williams was a strict disciplinarian and insisted that the inspectors treat all of the immigrants with fairness and kindness. Under his supervision, inspectors no longer detained wealthy immigrants in hope of bribing them. Immigrants were no longer held in filthy detention rooms while they waited for medical examinations or board of inquiry hearings. Food sellers and money changers (people who exchanged U.S. dollars for the currency of an immigrant's native country) were no longer allowed to charge exorbitant fees for their goods and services.

Williams's new policies fulfilled the American promise of liberty and freedom for millions of immigrants. His policies were continued by his successor, Robert Watchorn. In 1907, Ellis Island's busiest year, more than one million immigrants arrived at the station seeking out the American dream.

★ CHAPTER THREE

LEAVING THE OLD COUNTRY

As Ellis Island received its largest number of immigrant arrivals between 1901 and 1914, Europe was on the cusp of war. Most of the continent was divided into four autocratic empires (large states each ruled by a single individual with absolute power): Germany, Russia, the Austro-Hungarian Empire, and the Ottoman Empire (now modern-day Turkey), all in constant turmoil over land and political control.

The immigrants on the steerage deck of the *Germanic* are pictured in this sketch as their ship passes the Statue of Liberty.

Each of these empires included multiethnic populations that practiced a number of different religions. These diverse peoples were forced to conform to the cultures and beliefs of their tyrannical governments. Religious persecution, economic depression, and political rebellion drove many Europeans to seek refuge in the United States. Some young men left Europe to avoid being drafted into the army, which in czarist Russia required a commitment of up to twenty-five years of service. Many families came to America to escape the crippling poverty and food shortages typical of rural life in their eastern European villages. Thousands of Russian Jews fled pogroms—organized riots that left Jewish businesses and homes looted and burned and thousands of Jews dead.

Immigrants often had to work day and night to save the money for the voyage. The trip itself might require traveling for months on foot or by wagon, train, boat, and ship, moving ever westward toward America. At the turn of the century, an adult ticket on a transatlantic steamship cost about $35.

UNACCOMPANIED MINORS

Often, children traveled alone to meet parents who were already in America. These children were then sent to Ellis Island to appear before a board of "special inquiry." An October 23, 1915, *New York Times* article describes the story of one boy, aged nine, who traveled from England in a first-class cabin. Although his parents met him at the pier, he was taken to Ellis Island. Workers said it was the first time they had seen a child so young sent to the board when the parents were there to meet him.

Children were charged half that price, and infants traveled for free. Some borrowed the money from relatives. Others sold almost all of their belongings. Often, families were separated for years at a time so that fathers, husbands, and brothers could start to make a life in America and send money home to the "old country" to support their families and save up for their relatives' eventual journeys to the United States.

AN UNCOMFORTABLE VOYAGE

Though steamship companies often advertised a travel time of six days, the trip across the Atlantic could take anywhere from ten days to one month. Immigrants traveled in steerage, the lowest class of accommodation on board.

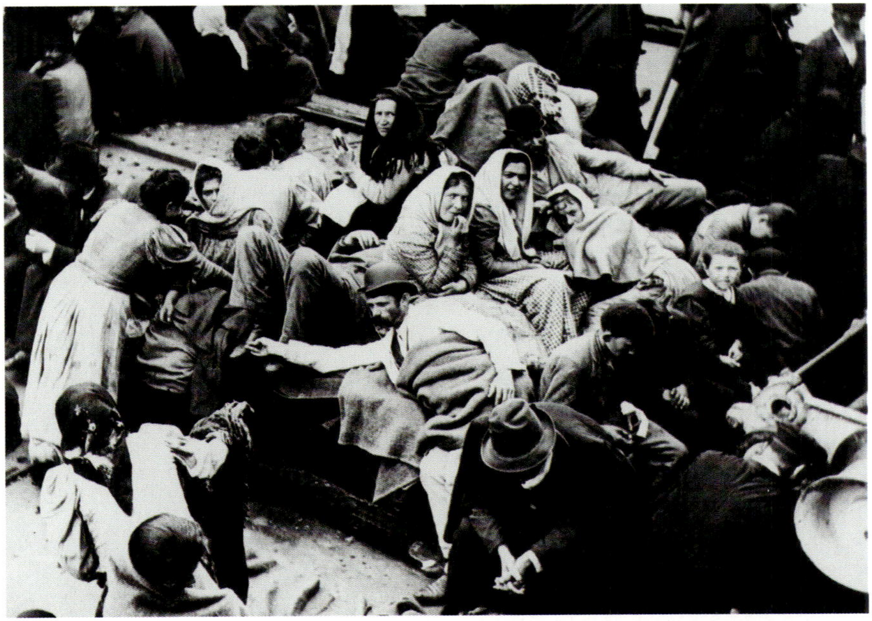

Photographer Jacob Riis lived on the Lower East Sice and examined life there through photography. This image was taken of steerage passengers getting a rare breath of fresh air on board a ship arriving at Ellis Island.

Deep in the hull of the ship, without portholes or decks, the immigrants were crowded into a single, large room. A blanket hung over a rope divided the room down the center and separated the men from the women and children. The ceiling was only 6 or 8 feet (2 or 2.5 meters) high.

Beds, stacked two or three high, lined the walls. Thin, lice-infested mattresses provided little comfort, but those immigrants who traveled with their own feather bedding found the sleeping arrangements slightly more comfortable. Women with small children hoped to secure a lower bunk. These mothers slept with their arms around their children so that they would not fall to the floor as the boat rocked and swayed on the waves.

Directly beneath them, the ship's engines thundered day and night. There was virtually no ventilation and bathroom facilities were inadequate. The stench of human waste was almost suffocating. There was little food, and the food that was offered, such as soggy bread and cured fish, was often inedible. Prepared travelers brought their own supply of food but more often than not, pangs of hunger went unanswered. During the day, the immigrants could enjoy fresh air on the upper decks. However, when the seas turned stormy, which they usually did at some point during the trip, the hatch to the lower deck was locked and tied, confining the steerage passengers to their dormitory-like room. Fresh water was available only on the upper deck, so during a storm, the steerage passengers went without. Many experienced severe seasickness and wondered if they would ever arrive in America.

ARRIVING IN AMERICA

Yet on that final day, when New York Harbor could be seen in the distance, the immigrants dressed themselves

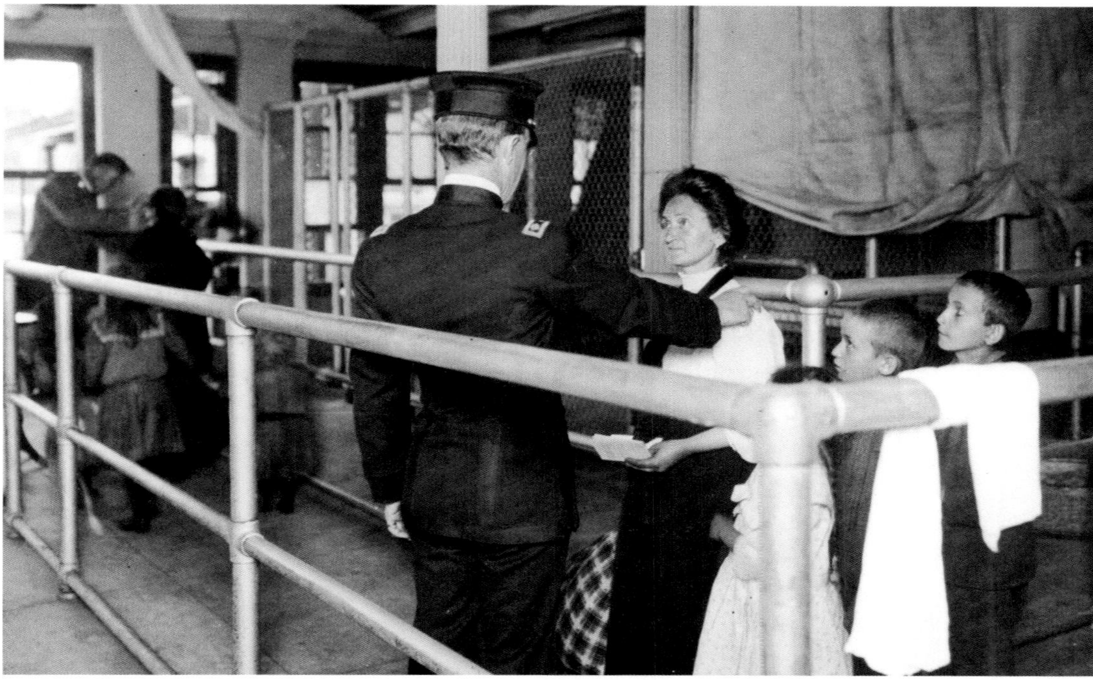

An immigration officer speaks with a female immigrant and her children.

and their children in their best clothes, often bundling up in two or three coats so that they had less to carry. They crowded the deck of the steamship as the city and the Statue of Liberty came into view—their first glimpse of America!

The ship docked at a pier on the Hudson River, and the first- and second-class passengers (usually American citizens and wealthier new immigrants) enjoyed a relatively quick inspection on board before debarking and dispersing to their destinations. Meanwhile the steerage passengers waited on board the steamship, sometimes for hours, before being transferred to the ferry that would take them to Ellis Island. Once they had crowded onto the ferry, however, it might not move from its mooring for hours. The immigrants, weighed down by layers of clothing, crying infants, and every kind of bulky luggage, were forced to stand on the open decks without food or water, wondering what would happen next.

As they waited, they gazed across the wide expanse of the Hudson River at Ellis Island. The station represented the last obstacle to freedom, to the beginning of a new life in America. Many immigrants looked with dread on the imposing structure, wondering whether or not the golden door would be opened to them.

★ CHAPTER FOUR

A ROUGH BEGINNING

The ferry deposited its cargo of weary new arrivals at the landing on Ellis Island. After such a long and exhausting journey, the welcome was often rougher and ruder than expected. The immigrants were herded off the ships and into lines, separated from family members, barked at by uniformed immigration officials, and occasionally swindled by dishonest porters and money changers and corrupt immigration officials. As wearying as the months of preparation had been before departure, as difficult as the ocean crossing was, the first few hours or days on Ellis Island would often prove the hardest part of an immigrant's journey.

KEEPING TRACK OF PASSENGERS

According to legislation passed in 1893, steamship captains were required to provide passenger manifests, or lists, detailing the particulars of each immigrant, including marital status, occupation, final destination, and political affiliation. Lawmakers

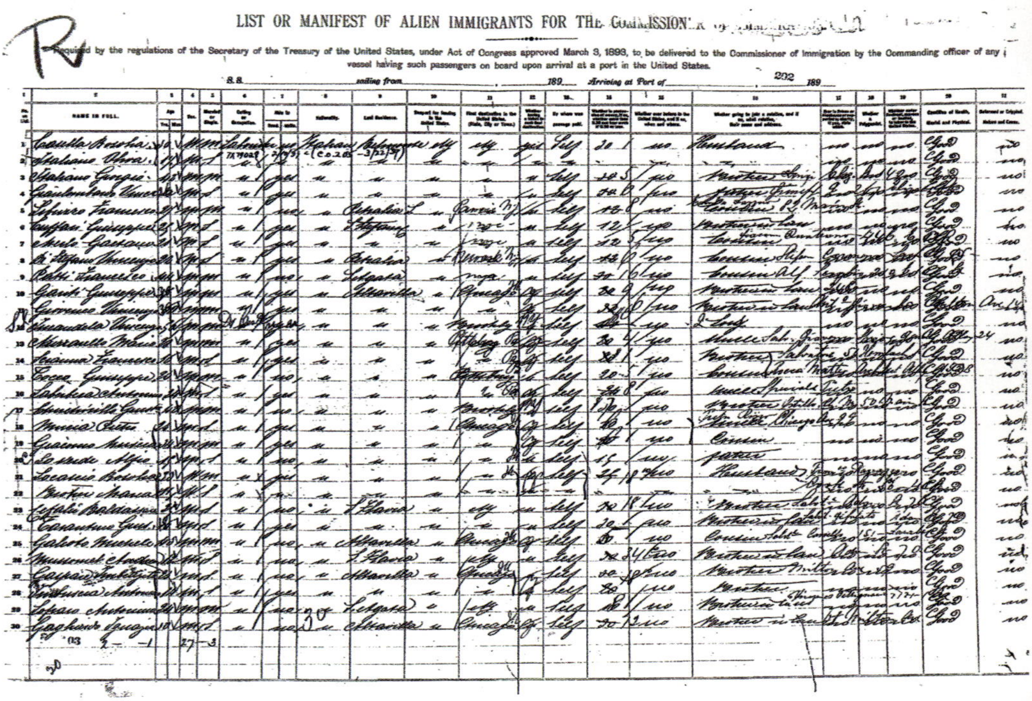

LIST OR MANIFEST OF ALIEN IMMIGRANTS FOR THE COMMISSIONER OF IMMIGRATION

Required by the regulations of the Secretary of the Treasury of the United States, under Act of Congress approved March 3, 1893, to be delivered to the Commissioner of Immigration by the Commanding officer of any vessel having such passengers on board upon arrival at a port in the United States.

A ship's manifest pages detailed passengers on board and their points of embarkation and disembarkation, as well as any notes from the captain, including medical ones.

believed that this policy would help reduce ticket sales at an immigrant's port of origin. Because steamship companies had to pay for the return voyages of rejected and deported immigrants, steamship ticket agents would conduct preliminary inspections when creating the manifests and refuse to sell tickets to those immigrants who would almost certainly be rejected once they reached America.

As a result, all immigrants who passed through the main doors of Ellis Island carried slips of paper bearing their manifest numbers, often pinned to their dresses or coats. Arranged in groups according to their manifest numbers, they passed under a crowded iron and glass canopy and through the doors of the main building.

MEDICAL SCREENING

Herded up a staircase, the immigrants were next ushered through the medical inspection line. Most assumed that the medical inspection did not begin until they reached the doctor at the end of the line, but as the immigrants stood waiting they were already being observed and screened by doctors standing discreetly off to the side. The immigrants passed through a small, railed maze that forced them to turn at right angles to the unnoticed examiners, allowing the doctors to observe from various angles. These doctors noted the way the immigrants walked, the quality of their complexions, and their general demeanors to try to identify any obvious signs of disease or disability.

Immigrants in line for inspections in 1920

Once the immigrants reached the examining doctor at the end of the long line, special attention was paid to their eyes, hands, and throat, where infections could be developing and symptoms of illness could be detected. Trachoma, an eye disease, and favus, a skin disease, were common, contagious, and difficult to treat. Both diseases were grounds for immediate deportation. The immigrants were also given stamped identification cards, giving the doctors the opportunity to test the immigrants' eyesight.

CODES FOR SICK IMMIGRANTS

Illness Code	Illness or Area of Illness
B	back problems
C	conjunctivitis
Ct	trachoma
E	eyes
F	face
Ft	foot issue
G	goiter
H	heart problems
K	hernia
L	lameness
N	neck
P	physical and lungs
Pg	pregnancy
S	senility
Sc	scalp
X (placed high on the right shoulder)	suspected mental defect
X (placed lower on the right shoulder)	disease or deformity
X within a circle	definite mental defect

Those immigrants who were thought to have physical or mental deficiencies were herded into caged enclosures, their coats marked in code with chalk, indicating the reason for their detainment. If they were ill, they would be hospitalized in one of the station's hospital units and detained during their convalescence. A board of inquiry would review their medical conditions and determine if they would be allowed to remain in the United States or be forced to return to their homeland.

THE INSPECTORS' EXAMINATION

Having undergone the medical inspection, those immigrants found to be healthy joined the lines that led to the desks of the immigration inspectors. Here they might wait for hours before coming before the man who would decide their fate. The immigration inspectors spent about two minutes with each immigrant, asking a series of questions based on the information printed in the ship's manifest. Because immigrants had heard about this phase of the process from relatives and friends who had immigrated earlier, they were often prepared for these questions and were able to deliver well-rehearsed answers. In later years, inspectors also administered literacy tests in the immigrants' native languages.

The immigration inspector's examination was full of drama and anxiety for the hopeful immigrant. When the inspector asked the immigrant whether he had a job awaiting him at his final destination, the temptation to answer "Yes" was strong. The immigrant instinctively wanted to demonstrate that he could support himself and his family and would not become a burden to society. It was in his best interest to answer "No." Coming to America for the purpose of working for a specific business on a specific job was in violation of the 1885 Alien

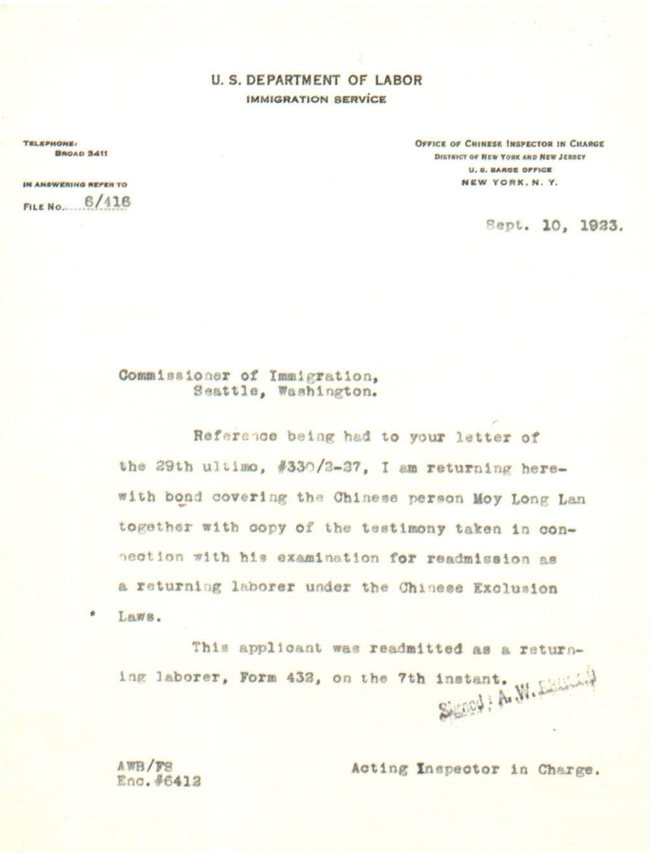

U. S. DEPARTMENT OF LABOR
IMMIGRATION SERVICE

TELEPHONE: BROAD 3411

IN ANSWERING REFER TO
FILE No. 6/416

OFFICE OF CHINESE INSPECTOR IN CHARGE
DISTRICT OF NEW YORK AND NEW JERSEY
U. S. BARGE OFFICE
NEW YORK, N. Y.

Sept. 10, 1923.

Commissioner of Immigration,
Seattle, Washington.

Reference being had to your letter of the 29th ultimo, #330/3-37, I am returning herewith bond covering the Chinese person Moy Long Lan together with copy of the testimony taken in connection with his examination for readmission as a returning laborer under the Chinese Exclusion Laws.

This applicant was readmitted as a returning laborer, Form 432, on the 7th instant.

Signed: A. W. [illegible]

Acting Inspector in Charge.

AWB/FS
Enc. #6412

A September 10, 1923, letter regarding Chinese immigrant Moy Long, who had successfully requested re-entry to the United States. The Act to Prohibit the Coming of Chinese Persons into the United States (the Geary Act) was passed in May 1892 and extended in 1902. Chinese laborers had to register and provide a certificate proving they had a right to be in the country. (For a transcription, see page 53.)

Contract Labor Law. Somehow, however, the immigrant had to prove that he did not have a job already lined up but that he could find one easily if given the opportunity and not become dependent on government aid soon after leaving Ellis Island.

DETENTION ON THE ISLAND

Immigrants were detained for many reasons—personal, political, and economic. Those without money or immediate means to support themselves but with promises of aid from friends or relatives were often held until money was sent to them at the island or concerned relatives could come and defend their application for entry. This was often the case for women and children whose husbands and fathers awaited them in the United States. If at the end of five days money or help had not arrived, poor and unsupported immigrants were given the choice of being deported or being turned over to the care of an American charitable organization.

If the government of an immigrant's native country warned U.S. officials that he or she was a convicted criminal, entry into the United States was denied. A member of a local labor union might inform immigration officials that an immigrant's journey had been paid for by his contracted employer, thereby violating the 1885 Alien Contract Labor Law. A deserted wife might alert authorities to the identity of her missing, runaway husband. Inspectors also detained immigrants they suspected of being prostitutes, polygamists, or supporters of certain unpopular or radical political views (such as Communism). Most often, however, immigrants were detained for one primary reason—money. Many were not permitted to leave the island and finally enter the United States until they could prove they would not become a public charge or dependent on private charity.

Having been declared unfit for entry, immigrants might return to their country of origin aboard the very ship on which they arrived in the United States. More often, however, they were held at Ellis Island for one or two weeks before a ship bound for their homeland made a scheduled departure. If they appealed the inspector's decision, they might enter into a lengthy legal proceeding, extending their stay at Ellis Island by weeks.

Detention on the island was often quite unpleasant, especially during the station's busiest years, between 1901 and 1914 (after which reforms greatly improved daily life for the internees). The aliens were crowded into locked dormitories or hospital wards. The dormitories were lice-infested and cramped, offering accommodations that immigrants compared unfavorably to Siberian prison camps and hell itself. The detainees met several times each day to enjoy hearty meals free of charge in the cafeteria-style dining halls but were otherwise left to entertain themselves. Families generally met only at meals, and the outdoors were enjoyed only on the tar-covered rooftops of the lower buildings.

About 20 percent of all arrivals were temporarily detained at Ellis Island, while the rest were permitted to enter the country. Of those detained, only a small percentage were eventually excluded and deported. In 1914, for example, 878,052 immigrants were admitted at Ellis Island, and 175,580 immigrants were detained. Of the detainees, 16,588, or about 2 percent, were deported. Millions of other immigrants continued on downstairs, where they met

An interior view of the Great Hall at the Ellis Island Immigration Station around 1910

relatives or friends and boarded the ferry bound for lower Manhattan or the barges that would carry them to railroad stations in New Jersey.

A NEW LIFE IN AMERICA

As difficult as the journey that lay behind the immigrants was, what lay ahead, in cities and towns across America, was an even greater challenge: creating a new life in America. Immigrants of all nationalities and from all walks of life faced discrimination and hostility. Many lived in squalor in the crowded tenements that lined the streets of ethnic neighborhoods. Thousands labored long hours in the dangerous working conditions of the stockyards and sweatshops of the major urban slums. Some fell victim to swindles, losing what little money they had to con men.

Many reacted to the anxieties of their new life by seeking comfort in their cultural traditions. They joined ethnic organizations, read foreign-language newspapers, and did not stray far from their neighborhoods where many of their former countrymen and countrywomen also lived. Others struggled to strike a better balance between maintaining the traditions of their native culture and becoming active members of the larger American society. They would become assimilated—absorbed into the dynamic, multiethnic culture bubbling all around them. Their new status as American citizens would become at least as important to their identity as their ethnic heritage was.

As new immigrants assimilated to life in America, they saved and sent money back for relatives to join them, bringing more and more new Americans. But two world wars turned the tidal wave of immigrants to a trickle.

★ CHAPTER FIVE

WAR STEMS THE TIDE

Political tensions between opposing empires in eastern and southern Europe came to a head in June 1914 with the assassination of the archduke of Austria, Franz Ferdinand. A month later, the Austro-Hungarians declared war. In weeks, most of Europe was embroiled in battle in the first conflict to be called total war.

FROM GATEWAY TO PRISON

The immigrant traffic at Ellis Island reduced to a trickle. The busiest immigration ports of Europe, such as Hamburg and Bremen in Germany, were blockaded by the British navy. Commercial traffic, including immigrant steamships, was barred from the high seas, where submarine warfare was fierce and civilian ships were threatened with attack. Those immigrants who wished to come to the United States could not, and those who had hoped to return to Europe after a few years in America were also disappointed. In 1915, Ellis Island saw only 178,416 new arrivals. This

German prisoners of war stand with armed U.S. soldiers in 1918.

number continued to decline, reaching a low of 28,867 three years later.

In April 1917, the United States was finally drawn into World War I, three years after the conflict first broke out. Ellis Island was immediately transformed into a holding cell for two thousand German prisoners of war (POWs), primarily the crews of German ships moored in New York Harbor. The island was placed under military guard. A stockade (protective fence or enclosure) was built around the power plant to guard against sabotage. Floodlights were placed on all of the buildings to help prevent prisoner escapes.

As Ellis Island was being transformed into a prisoner of war camp, the federal Department of Justice and other smaller government agencies became increasingly aggressive in their efforts to deport resident aliens (noncitizens living legally in the United States) suspected of various crimes, especially those accused of being Communist sympathizers or revolutionaries. These people were labeled spies and saboteurs, and they were carefully guarded. Because there were no ships departing for Europe, however, these accused criminals had to be housed at Ellis Island with the German POWs.

In the spring of 1917, as the United States entered the war, a new immigration law went into effect. The 1917 Immigration Act, which had been rejected by President Woodrow Wilson but revived when Congress overrode the president's veto, repealed all previous immigration legislation that contradicted its detailed provisions. It specified thirty-two separate groups of undesirable immigrants, including among the excluded all those immigrants who could not read and write, the mentally challenged, alcoholics, epileptics, criminals, the handicapped, polygamists, revolutionaries, the impoverished, and the physically or mentally ill. The passage of this restrictive immigration law signaled to the world that America was closing its borders. Its gates were no longer opened wide for the world's immigrants.

With immigration being choked off, Ellis Island's role continued to change and evolve. In 1918, the island's German POWs and accused alien criminals were transferred to internment camps elsewhere in the United States. The sick immigrants were turned over to private hospitals, and the medical facilities at the island were put in the hands of the army's medical department. The dormitories were turned into barracks and occupied by American soldiers. The bureau of immigration was required to do most of its inspections of new arrivals on board ships, not even allowing the immigrants to step foot on the island. Ellis Island—once the gateway to America for the world's hopeful masses—was now transformed into a military headquarters with the primary purpose of keeping people out.

THE WAR COMES TO ELLIS ISLAND

In 1917 when the United States entered World War I, Ellis Island was used as a navy way station. The hospital building was used for wounded servicemen, and enemy combatants were detained on the island. The Department of Justice also used Ellis Island as a deportation site for Bolshevik aliens who were sent back to Russia.

WORSENING CONDITIONS FOR IMMIGRANTS

With the end of World War I, Europe was transformed. Its once mighty imperial armies had been ravaged by war, and many people now lived in extreme poverty. Its borders had been radically redrawn and its old regimes had been toppled, while new governments stood in their place and new countries emerged on its territories. This state of chaos and uncertainty made the United States a desirable destination once again, and interest in immigration increased.

Americans' interest in welcoming immigrants, however, had greatly decreased. Though the war was fought on European soil, Americans, too, had lost sons and husbands in the war and had experienced the sacrifices of wartime shortages. Many of them came to distrust foreigners and radicals, whom they blamed for the recent war. In large numbers, Americans turned their attention to the enemy that might be lurking in their own backyard, the democracy-hating revolutionary who was suspected of trying to turn America into a Communist society. In the coming year, a series of labor strikes and random bombings, incorrectly blamed on Communist radicals, fueled their fear and anger.

Just weeks before the October 16, 1918, armistice that put an end to fighting in Europe, Congress passed legislation that made it much easier to deport any resident alien suspected of being an anarchist or a Communist. Public hysteria, known as the Red Scare (red was the color associated with Communist revolution), gripped the country, and over the next year many accused radicals were deported. The army and navy evacuated Ellis Island in 1919, and the station prepared to handle the outgoing flood of suspected "Reds." Mass deportations of suspected revolutionaries followed, with many of the detainees passing through Ellis Island on their way back to Europe.

In time, the Red Scare subsided, though it would resurface again in the late 1940s and gain great strength in the 1950s with the beginning of the Cold War between the United States and the Soviet Union. During the lull, Ellis Island returned to the business of processing new arrivals.

By 1920, the number of new arrivals was again on the rise. Ellis Island welcomed 225,206 immigrants that year. Once again, New York Harbor was crowded with arrivals, and passengers had to wait for hours to be ferried to the island and examined in the registry hall. The dining halls, meant to seat eight hundred each, were again crowded with three thousand people in each hall at every meal. This overcrowding was partly because the immigrants were given more rigorous and time-consuming examinations, as required under law by the 1917 immigration act. Literacy tests were administered. Each immigrant also received an extensive medical exam. Throughout this period, all arrivals were deloused to protect against typhus, a severe bacterial disease carried by body lice and causing fever, rash, headaches, and delirium. Their baggage and clothes were also taken from them to be disinfected as a precaution.

As if the rigorous and often humiliating screenings and examinations were not difficult enough on the immigrants, the facilities on Ellis Island were falling into severe disrepair. Most observers agreed that the living quarters were filthy, cramped, and infested with vermin. The island was extremely understaffed and overworked, and the immigrants were often mistreated. They slept on blankets laid on the floor because there were never enough beds. They were herded like animals from one room to the next and denied any privacy. Even the buildings themselves were crumbling.

A 2012 photograph of the dormitory in Ellis Island hospital, one of the last buildings to be renovated

NEW IMMIGRATION LAWS

With the sudden increase in immigration levels in the early 1920s, the voices of those in favor of stricter immigration policies were once again heard. The beginning of an economic recession early in the decade roused the Knights of Labor to again demand stricter controls. The postwar European typhus epidemic was another cause of concern among several influential health commissioners. In response, the House of Representatives proposed suspending immigration for one year. No new aliens would be allowed to enter while the government worked out a plan for dealing with the increasing numbers of people seeking refuge in America. In the end, both houses of Congress enacted what has come to be called the First Quota Act, effective June 3, 1921.

The First Quota Act was intended as a temporary solution to the country's immigration woes, but it soon became the basis for American immigration law until 1965. The law stated that each foreign country would be allowed only a certain number of immigrants to be admitted to the United States. Each country's quota would be set at 3 percent of the population of that nationality living in the United States during the 1910 census. For example, the number of Italians admitted to the United States in 1923 could not exceed 3 percent of the number of foreign-born Italians living in the United States in 1910. In addition, the quota was spread out over the year, so that no more than 20 percent of the annual quota could be admitted in any given month. Finally, the law said that the total number of immigrants admitted to the United States in a single year under the quota system could not exceed 358,000. Once that number of immigrants had arrived in the United States, all immigration for that year would cease, even if

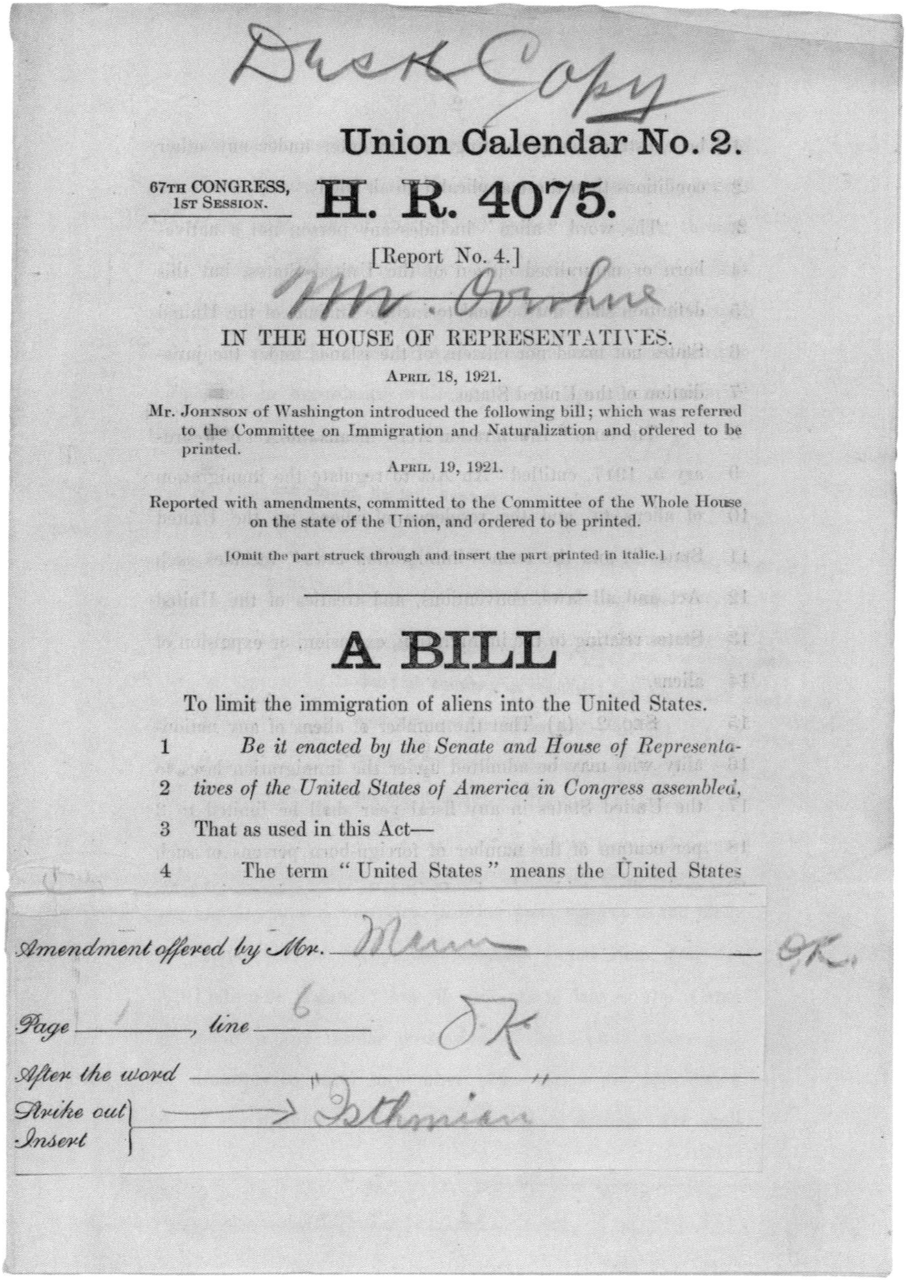

Desk Copy

Union Calendar No. 2.

67TH CONGRESS, 1ST SESSION.

H. R. 4075.

[Report No. 4.]

IN THE HOUSE OF REPRESENTATIVES.

APRIL 18, 1921.

Mr. JOHNSON of Washington introduced the following bill; which was referred to the Committee on Immigration and Naturalization and ordered to be printed.

APRIL 19, 1921.

Reported with amendments, committed to the Committee of the Whole House on the state of the Union, and ordered to be printed.

[Omit the part struck through and insert the part printed in italic.]

A BILL

To limit the immigration of aliens into the United States.

Be it enacted by the Senate and House of Representatives of the United States of America in Congress assembled, That as used in this Act—

The term "United States" means the United States

Amendment offered by Mr. ______ O.K.

Page 1, *line* 6 OK

After the word ______

Strike out → "Isthmian"

Insert

A copy of what became the First Quota Act. An increase in immigrants from southern and eastern Europe led Americans to support restrictive immigration. (For a transcription, see page 53.)

foreign countries had not yet reached their quota. Given that more than a million immigrants used to be admitted every year, these regulations dealt a crushing blow to thousands of hopeful European immigrants.

In the spring of 1924, Congress passed the Second Quota Act, which was to go into effect the following year. The new law set each foreign nation's quota at 2 percent of the population of its former citizens living in the United States in 1890, further reducing the potential number of admitted immigrants. It also set the total number of admitted aliens per year at 164,000, down from 358,000. Finally, and most important, the law required European immigrants to obtain visas from the American consuls located in their countries of origin. To so do involved undergoing a thorough examination akin to those performed at Ellis Island. This measure was intended to prevent undesirable immigrants from spending their time and money to make the transatlantic voyage only to be rejected by the inspectors at Ellis Island. The Second Quota Act served its purpose; immigration at Ellis Island was sharply reduced. On an average day, only three hundred immigrants arrived at the station.

Shortly after the law took effect, the surgeon general of the United States suggested employing medical examiners at all of the U.S. consuls overseas to further curb the rate of immigrants who were deported for medical reasons. This was done, and the examiners performed thorough exams on all potential immigrants before visas were issued. Eventually immigration inspectors were added to the staffs of overseas consuls, ensuring that all transatlantic passengers were "preprocessed" before reaching Ellis Island. Under this new system, a visa came to guarantee entrance into the United States.

As a result, the primary function of immigration stations such as Ellis Island—to review immigrants and determine whether they should be admitted—was made unnecessary. All of the screening was now taking place at an immigrant's point of departure—his or her home country—rather than in an immigration station in the United States.

THE GATES CLOSE

By 1928, Ellis Island was viewed by many as a hulking, expensive, obsolete institution. Yet it remained in service, even during the darkest hours of the stock market crash of 1929 and the prolonged depression that followed throughout the 1930s. Because the United States was suffering such a severe economic crisis, it no longer looked to foreigners like the land of opportunity. During this period, immigration was nearly nonexistent. So Ellis Island began to be used mainly as a deportation center, as the Justice Department and other federal agencies focused on expelling illegal aliens. Other foreign-born residents left gladly, at the government's expense, to escape the desperate economic conditions facing America.

Meanwhile, in Europe, totalitarian regimes were again taking hold. Though a strong minority of voices spoke up in favor of offering American refuge to German and Austrian Jews living under Adolf Hitler's Third Reich, the anti-immigration faction in Congress defeated proposals to loosen entry laws. In 1940, the Nazis invaded Norway and France. In response, the U.S. State Department, afraid Nazi spies would infiltrate America disguised as refugees, ordered American consuls overseas to tighten their restrictions on visas. All told, perhaps only 250,000 European refugees seeking asylum were admitted to the United States during World War II.

By the late 1930s, the immigrant had ceased to be viewed as an imported good, a potential labor force, or a charity case. As the United States prepared to enter World War II, the immigrant was viewed only as a threat to national security. The Alien Registration Act of June 1940 required all resident aliens to be registered and all arriving immigrants to be fingerprinted. During the war, Ellis Island—in particular the baggage and dormitory building—once again served as a detention center for seamen from enemy nations and suspected criminals. The U.S. Coast Guard also used the island as a training center.

Following the end of World War II, Ellis Island would see a final flurry of immigration activity in 1950—mostly the processing and housing of detainees and deportees—with the passage of the Internal Security Act, which excluded members of Communist and fascist organizations from entering the United States. From then on, Ellis Island ceased to function as a working immigration station. The dilapidated buildings continued to house the offices of the Immigration and Naturalization Service until 1955 when the island was vacated. The Ellis Island ferry remained permanently moored.

★ CHAPTER SIX

A NEW DAY FOR ELLIS ISLAND

Ellis Island lay abandoned for many years. A lone caretaker and his bulldog were left to guard the island, but robbers took the few furnishings that were left behind. Buildings were water-damaged, overgrown by weeds, and infested by birds.

When the nation again turned its attention to the dilapidated structures, various proposals were made to turn the island into a park and recreation center, a resort, a home for the elderly, a rehabilitation center for alcoholics, and even a liberal arts college. These recommendations were eventually all rejected. Instead, on May 11, 1965, President Lyndon B. Johnson declared that Ellis Island would become part of the Statue of Liberty National Monument, operated by the National Park Service. During the ceremony that unveiled this plan, Johnson also announced his proposed immigration bill, which would repeal the anti-immigration policies of the First and Second Quota Acts.

Between 1976 and 1984, Ellis Island was open to the public on a limited basis. During this time, an

President Lyndon Johnson speaks after signing the new immigration bill into law at the foot of the Statue of Liberty, October 3, 1965. (For a transcription of President Johnson's speech, see page 54.)

in-depth history of the immigration station was made, and architectural proposals were presented for its renovation. In 1984, after nearly twenty years of debate and disagreement, the island was temporarily closed to the public, and the massive reconstruction project began. After six years and $160 million worth of careful restoration, the Ellis Island Immigration Museum—housed in the former main building—was opened to the public on September 10, 1990. The structure was restored to look as it did between 1918 and 1924. The iron and glass canopy was redesigned, and a restaurant patio was added, but the structures were otherwise restored to all of their former glory.

Visitors to the newly opened Ellis Island Immigration Museum are shown here in October 2013.

Displays document the role Ellis Island played in the immigrant experience, as well as offer a larger view of the four-hundred-year history of immigration to America. The museum includes personal objects and artifacts, vintage desks and benches, documents, photographs, prints, videos, documentary films, interactive displays, historical reenactments of actual hearings for arrivals who failed inspection, and the oral histories of immigrants. An American Immigrant Wall of Honor lists the names of more than six hundred thousand individuals who immigrated to America, and more names are continuously added. The museum also features the American Family Immigration History Center, a

FROM IMMIGRATION CENTER TO MONUMENT

A visitor looks at one of the art installations at the Peopling of America Center at the Ellis Island Immigration Museum.

In 1965, President Lyndon B. Johnson made Ellis Island a part of the Statue of Liberty National Monument. A clean-up campaign was organized and in 1976 the island opened for public tours. Restoration of the island cost $160 million and began in 1986. The island reopened in 1990. Since then, the property has been updated and new centers have been opened, such as the American Family Immigration History Center (2001) and the Peopling of America Center (2011, 2015).

research facility that contains ships' records for more than twenty-two million people who passed through Ellis Island from 1892 to 1924.

A trip to the Ellis Island Immigration Museum is an extraordinary experience, one that almost two million visitors a year enjoy. Since the vast majority of Americans are descended from immigrants or are immigrants themselves, the museum offers a unique connection to America's shared past. It allows visitors to explore their own family histories and achieve a greater appreciation for the experiences of their fellow citizens. It provokes the realization in viewers that for no matter how many generations their families have lived in the United States, they are almost certainly related to someone who was a bewildered newcomer, a foreigner, frightened and hopeful, just looking for an opportunity to make a life for him- or herself in a free country.

Ellis Island stands as a testament to America's mixed heritage and as a monument to the brave people who overcame tough obstacles, sacrificed, and faced uncertainty in search of a new life.

TIMELINE

1630 The governors of Nieuw Amsterdam (New Amsterdam, later New York) buy the 3.5-acre (1.4 ha) island.

1776 The island is now owned by merchant Samuel Ellis.

1808 The family of Samuel Ellis sells the island in New York Harbor that he owned to New York State. The U.S. government buys Ellis Island from New York State for $10,000 later that year.

1813 Fort Gibson is built on Ellis Island, housing a large store of ammunition.

1861 Fort Gibson is dismantled.

1890 Ellis Island is chosen as the site for a new federal immigration station for the port of New York.

1892 The Ellis Island Immigration Center opens on January 1.

1897 Wooden immigration buildings are destroyed by fire.

1900 The Ellis Island Immigration Center reopens. The new buildings are made of brick and stone.

1907 Roughly 1.25 million immigrants pass through Ellis Island, more than any other year.

1924 Immigration through Ellis Island begins to wane.

1943 Ellis Island is transformed into a detention center for enemy POWs and aliens.

1954 Ellis Island is closed.

1965 Lyndon Johnson announces that Ellis Island will become part of the National Park Service.

1974 The Restore Ellis Island Committee is formed to raise money for renovations.

1983 Restoration on Ellis Island's main building begins.

1990 The Ellis Island Immigration Museum opens on September 10.

2001 The American Family Immigration History Center opens.

2011 The Peopling of America Center, a museum that explores arrivals before the era of Ellis Island, opens.

2015 The second phase of the Peopling of America Center opens.

PAGE 32: LETTER FROM THE INSPECTOR IN CHARGE TO THE COMMISSIONER OF IMMIGRATION, SEATTLE, WASHINGTON REGARDING MOY LONG

U.S. Department of Labor
Immigration Services
Telephone: Broad 3411

Office of Chinese Inspector in Charge
District of New York and New Jersey
U.S. Barge Office
New York, N.Y.

In Answering Refer To
File No. 6/416

Sept. 10, 1923

Commissioner of Immigration,
Seattle, Washington.

Reference being had to your letter of the 29th ultimo, #330/2-27, I am returning herewith bond covering the Chinese person Moy Long Lan together with copy of the testimony taken in connection with his examination for readmission as a returning laborer under the Chinese Exclusion Laws.

This applicant was readmitted as a returning laborer, Form 432, on the 7th instant.

AWB/FS
Enc. #6412

Acting Inspector in Charge.
Signed A.W. [...]

PAGE 43: EXCERPT FROM A DESK COPY OF THE BILL PRESENTED IN THE HOUSE OF REPRESENTATIVES THAT WOULD BECOME THE FIRST QUOTA ACT

IN THE HOUSE OF REPRESENTATIVES.
April 18, 1921.
Mr. Johnson of Washington introduced the following bill; which was referred to the Committee on Immigration and Naturalization and ordered to be printed.

A BILL

To limit the immigration of aliens into the United States.

Be it enacted by the Senate and House of Representatives of the United States of America in Congress assembled, That as used in this Act—

The term "United States" means the United States, and any waters, territory, or other place subject to the jurisdiction thereof except the Canal Zone and the Philippine Islands; but if any alien leaves the Canal Zone or any insular possession of the United States and attempts to enter any other place under the jurisdiction of the United States nothing contained in this Act shall be construed as permitting him to enter under any other conditions than those applicable to all aliens.

The word "alien" includes any person not a native-born or naturalized citizen of the United States, but this definition shall not be held to include Indians of the United States not taxed nor citizens of the islands under the jurisdiction of the United States.

The term "Immigration Act" means the Act of February 5, 1917, entitled "An Act to regulate the immigration of aliens to, and the residence of aliens in, the United States"; and the term "immigration laws" includes such Act and all laws, conventions, and treaties of the United States relating to the immigration, exclusion, or expulsion of aliens.

Sec. 2. (a) That the number of aliens of any nationality who may be admitted under the immigration laws to the United States in any fiscal year shall be limited to 3 per centum of the number of foreign born persons of such nationality resident in the United States as determined by the United States census of 1910 . . .

PAGE 48: PRESIDENT LYNDON B. JOHNSON'S REMARKS AT THE SIGNING OF THE IMMIGRATION BILL, LIBERTY ISLAND, NEW YORK, OCTOBER 3, 1965

Mr. Vice President, Mr. Speaker, Mr. Ambassador Goldberg, distinguished Members of the leadership of the Congress, distinguished Governors and mayors, my fellow countrymen:

We have called the Congress here this afternoon not only to mark a very historic occasion, but to settle a very old issue that is in dispute. That issue is, to what congressional district does Liberty Island really belong—Congressman Farbstein or Congressman Gallagher? It will be settled by whoever of the two can walk first to the top of the Statue of Liberty.

This bill that we will sign today is not a revolutionary bill. It does not affect the lives of millions. It will not reshape the structure of our daily lives, or really add importantly to either our wealth or our power. Yet it is still one of the most important acts of this Congress and of this administration. For it does repair a very deep and painful flaw in the fabric of American justice. It corrects a cruel and enduring wrong in the conduct of the American Nation.

Speaker McCormack and Congressman Celler almost 40 years ago first pointed that out in their maiden speeches in the Congress. And this measure that we will sign today will really make us truer to ourselves both as a country and as a people. It will strengthen us in a hundred unseen ways.

I have come here to thank personally each Member of the Congress who labored so long and so valiantly to make this occasion come true today, and to make this bill a reality. I cannot mention all their names, for it would take much too long, but my gratitude--and that of this Nation--belongs to the 89th Congress.

We are indebted, too, to the vision of the late beloved President John Fitzgerald Kennedy, and to the support given to this measure by the then Attorney General and now Senator, Robert F. Kennedy.

In the final days of consideration, this bill had no more able champion than the present Attorney General, Nicholas Katzenbach, who, with New York's own "Manny" Celler, and Senator Ted Kennedy of Massachusetts, and Congressman Feighan of Ohio, and Senator Mansfield and Senator Dirksen constituting the leadership of the Senate, and Senator Javits, helped to guide this bill to passage, along with the help of the Members sitting in front of me today.

This bill says simply that from this day forth those wishing to immigrate to America shall be admitted on the basis of their skills and their close relationship to those already here.

This is a simple test, and it is a fair test. Those who can contribute most to this country—to its growth, to its strength, to its spirit—will be the first that are admitted to this land.

The fairness of this standard is so self-evident that we may well wonder that it has not always been applied. Yet the fact is that for over four decades the immigration policy of the United States has been twisted and has been distorted by the harsh injustice of the national origins quota system.

Under that system the ability of new immigrants to come to America depended upon the country of their birth. Only 3 countries were allowed to supply 70 percent of all the immigrants.

Families were kept apart because a husband or a wife or a child had been born in the wrong place.

Men of needed skill and talent were denied entrance because they came from southern or eastern Europe or from one of the developing continents.

This system violated the basic principle of American democracy—the principle that values and rewards each man on the basis of his merit as a man.

It has been un-American in the highest sense, because it has been untrue to the faith that brought thousands to these shores even before we were a country.

Today, with my signature, this system is abolished.

We can now believe that it will never again shadow the gate to the American Nation with the twin barriers of prejudice and privilege.

Our beautiful America was built by a nation of strangers. From a hundred different places or more they have poured forth into an empty land, joining and blending in one mighty and irresistible tide.

The land flourished because it was fed from so many sources—because it was nourished by so many cultures and traditions and peoples.

And from this experience, almost unique in the history of nations, has come America's attitude toward the rest of the world. We, because of what we are, feel safer and stronger in a world as varied as the people who make it up—a world where no country rules another and all countries can deal with the basic problems of human dignity and deal with those problems in their own way.

Now, under the monument which has welcomed so many to our shores, the American Nation returns to the finest of its traditions today.

The days of unlimited immigration are past.

But those who do come will come because of what they are, and not because of the land from which they sprung.

When the earliest settlers poured into a wild continent there was no one to ask them where they came from. The only question was: Were they sturdy enough to make the journey, were they strong enough to clear the land, were they enduring enough to make a home for freedom, and were they brave enough to die for liberty if it became necessary to do so?

And so it has been through all the great and testing moments of American history. Our history this year we see in Viet-Nam. Men there are dying—men named Fernandez and Zajac and Zelinko and Mariano and McCormick.

Neither the enemy who killed them nor the people whose independence they have fought to save ever asked them where they or their parents came from. They were all Americans. It was for free men and for America that they gave their all, they gave their lives and selves.

By eliminating that same question as a test for immigration the Congress proves ourselves worthy of those men and worthy of our own traditions as a Nation.

ASYLUM FOR CUBAN REFUGEES

So it is in that spirit that I declare this afternoon to the people of Cuba that those who seek refuge here in America will find it. The dedication of America to our traditions as an asylum for the oppressed is going to be upheld.

I have directed the Departments of State and Justice and Health, Education, and Welfare to immediately make all the necessary arrangements to permit those in Cuba who seek freedom to make an orderly entry into the United States of America.

Our first concern will be with those Cubans who have been separated from their children and their parents and their husbands and their wives and that are now in this country. Our next concern is with those who are imprisoned for political reasons.

And I will send to the Congress tomorrow a request for supplementary funds of $12,600,000 to carry forth the commitment that I am making today.

I am asking the Department of State to seek through the Swiss Government immediately the agreement of the Cuban Government in a request to the President of the International Red Cross Committee. The request is for the assistance of the Committee in processing the movement of refugees from Cuba to Miami. Miami will serve as a port of entry and a temporary stopping place for refugees as they settle in other parts of this country.

And to all the voluntary agencies in the United States, I appeal for their continuation and expansion of their magnificent work. Their help is needed in the reception and the settlement of those who choose to leave Cuba. The Federal Government will work closely with these agencies in their tasks of charity and brotherhood.

I want all the people of this great land of ours to know of the really enormous contribution which the compassionate citizens of Florida have made to humanity and to decency. And all States in this Union can join with Florida now in extending the hand of helpfulness and humanity to our Cuban brothers.

The lesson of our times is sharp and clear in this movement of people from one land to another. Once again, it stamps the mark of failure on a regime when many of its citizens voluntarily choose to leave the land of their birth for a more hopeful home in America. The future holds little hope for any government where the present holds no hope for the people.

And so we Americans will welcome these Cuban people. For the tides of history run strong, and in another day they can return to their homeland to find it cleansed of terror and free from fear.

Over my shoulders here you can see Ellis Island, whose vacant corridors echo today the joyous sound of long ago voices.

And today we can all believe that the lamp of this grand old lady is brighter today—and the golden door that she guards gleams more brilliantly in the light of an increased liberty for the people from all the countries of the globe.

Thank you very much.

GLOSSARY

armistice An end to war agreed upon by both sides.

army battery A grouping of large defensive guns.

assimilated Adopted the culture of the majority of people in a society.

asylum A place of refuge or shelter.

autocratic A government in which one person holds absolute power.

Bolshevik Any member of the political party that began to rule Russia in 1917.

cholera A deadly intestinal disease.

Communist In Russia, a member of the Social Democratic Party, or someone advocating the elimination of private property.

convalescence A period of recovery from illness or injury.

deport To send out of the country.

detainee A person held in legal custody.

dilapidated Broken down.

fortifications Defensive works.

garrison A military post.

nativist Someone who opposes immigration.

polygamist A person who is married to two or more people simultaneously.

public charge A person who is supported financially by the state and local government.

visa A document that verifies one's approval or endorsement by his or her native country.

FOR MORE INFORMATION

Ellis Island Immigration Museum
17 Battery Place 210
New York, NY 10004
(212) 561-4588
http://www.ellisisland.com
Located in the main building of the former immigration station, the museum is a restored monument to the immigrants who arrived in America through Ellis Island.

New-York Historical Society
170 Central Park West
New York, NY 10024
(212) 873-3400
http://www.nyhistory.org
The New-York Historical Society is a museum and library dedicated to historical research, art exhibitions, and public programs. It is the oldest museum in New York City.

Statue of Liberty—Ellis Island Foundation, Inc.
American Family Immigration History Center
292 Madison Avenue
New York, NY 10017
http://www.ellisisland.org
The Statue of Liberty—Ellis Island Foundation was created to restore both of these national monuments and remains today for the upkeep of these monuments for millions of visitors per year.

WEBSITES

Because of the changing nature of Internet links, Rosen Publishing has developed an online list of websites related to the subject of this book. This site is updated regularly. Please use this link to access this list:

http://www.rosenlinks.com/UAH/Ellis

FOR FURTHER READING

Demuth, Patricia Brennan. *What Was Ellis Island?* New York, NY: Penguin Publishing Group, 2014.

Freedman, Russell. *Immigrant Kids*. New York, NY: Penguin Young Readers Group, 1999.

Hunsicker, Kelley. *Chinese Immigrants in America: An Interactive History Adventure*. North Mankato, MN: Capstone Press, 2008.

Kenney, Karen Latchanna. *Our Nation's Pride: Ellis Island*. Edina, MN: ABDO Publishing Company, 2011.

Lawlor, Veronica. *I Was Dreaming to Come to America: Memories from the Ellis Island Oral History Project*. New York, NY: Penguin Goup, 2000.

Levine, Ellen. *If Your Name Was Changed at Ellis Island*. New York, NY: Scholastic, Inc., 1994.

McDaniel, Melissa. *Cornerstones of Freedom: Ellis Island*. New York, NY: Scholastic Library Publishing, 2011.

Raatma, Lucia. *Ellis Island.* North Mankato, MN: Capstone Press, 2007.

Raum, Elizabeth. *German Immigrants in America: An Interactive History Adventure*. North Mankato, MN: Capstone Press, 2008.

Raum, Elizabeth. *Irish Immigrants in America: An Interactive History Adventure*. North Mankato, MN: Capstone Press, 2007.

Sandler, Martin. *Island of Hope: The Story of Ellis Island and the Journey to America*. New York, NY: Scholastic, Inc., 2004.

Szucs, Loretto Dennis. *Ellis Island: Tracing Your Family History Through America's Gateway*. Salt Lake City: Ancestry Publishing, 2001.

BIBLIOGRAPHY

"About Ellis Island." The Statue of Liberty-Ellis Island Foundation, Inc. Retrieved October 20, 2014 (http://www.libertyellisfoundation.org/about-the-ellis-island).

Anbinder, Tyler. *Five Points*. New York, NY: The Free Press, 2001.

Barkan, Elliott Robert. *Immigrants in American History: Arrival, Adaptation, and Integration*. Santa Barbara, CA: ABC-CLIO, 2013.

Briggs, Vernon M., Jr. *Mass Immigration and the National Interest*. Armonk, NY: M. E. Sharpe, Inc., 1992.

Brownstone, David M., Irene Franck, and Douglass L. Brownstone. *Island of Hope, Island of Tears*. New York, NY: Metro Books, 2002.

Daniels, Roger. *Coming to America: A History of Immigration and Ethnicity in American Life*. New York, NY: Harper Perennial Library, 2002.

Dinnerstein, Leonard, and David M. Reimers. *Ethnic Americans*. New York, NY: Columbia University Press, 1999.

"Ellis Island." History.com. Retrieved October 20, 2014 (http://www.history.com/topics/ellis-island).

Fleegler, Robert L. *Ellis Island Nation: Immigration Policy and American Identity in the Twentieth Century*. Philadelphia, PA: University of Pennsylvania Press, 2013.

Jonas, Susan, ed. *Ellis Island: Echoes from a Nation's Past*. New York, NY: Aperture Foundation, 1997.

Pitkin, Thomas Monroe. *Keepers of the Gate*. New York, NY: New York University Press, 1975.

"Public Papers of the Presidents of the United States: Lyndon B. Johnson, 1965." Volume II, entry 546, pp. 1037-1040. Washington, DC: Government Printing Office, 1966.

Riis, Jacob A. *How the Other Half Lives: Studies Among the Tenements of New York*. New York, NY: Penguin USA, 1997.

Takaki, Ronald T. *A Different Mirror: A History of Multicultural America*. Boston, MA: Little, Brown & Co., 1994.

INDEX

ABOUT THE AUTHORS

Caitlin Merrick is a writer and historian. She lives in Trinidad, Colorado.

Gillian Houghton is an editor and writer in New York City.

PHOTO CREDITS

Cover Apic/Hulton Archive/Getty Images; p. 3 Lone Wolf Photography/Shutterstock.com; pp. 4–5 (background) Enigmangels/Shutterstock.com; p. 5 Hoberman/UIG/Bridgeman Images; p. 7 (inset) Archive Photos/Getty Images; pp. 7 (background), 14 (background), 21 (background), 27, 36, 47 Alessandro Colle/Shutterstock.com; p. 9 © North Wind Picture Archives; pp. 11, 21 (inset) Library of Congress Prints and Photographs Division; pp. 14 (inset), 32 National Archives and Records Administration; p. 17 Olaf Protze/Light Rocket/Getty Images; p. 18-19, 23 Courtesy National Park Service, Statue of Liberty National Monument; p. 25 Fotosearch/Archive Photos/Getty Images; p. 28 The Statue of Liberty-Ellis Island Foundation, Inc.; p. 29 Universal History Archive/Universal Images Group/Getty Images; p. 34 Interim Archives/Archive Photos/Getty Images; p. 37 Bain News Service/Buyenlarge/Archive Photos/Getty Images; p. 41 Ian Ference/Barcroft Media/Landov; p. 43 Records of the U.S. House of Representatives, National Archives and Records Administration; p. 48 Harry Benson/Express/Hulton Archive/Getty Images; p. 49 John Moore/Getty Images; p. 50 George Goodwin/SuperStock; cover, p. 1 design elements Piotr Krzeslak/Shutterstock.com (flag), Aleksandrs Bondars/Shutterstock.com (scroll); cover and interior pages background textures chudo-yudo/Shutterstock.com, Alina G/Shutterstock.com, Attitude/Shutterstock.com, sl_photo/Shutterstock.com

Designer: Michael Moy; Editor: Tracey Baptiste